Ellie the Guitar Fairy

ISBN: 978-0-545-10625-2

12 11 10 9 8 7 6 5 4 3 2 10 11 12 13 14 15/0

Printed in the U.S.A.

First Scholastic Printing, January 2010

Ellie the Guitar Fairy

by Daisy Meadows

SCHOLASTIC INC.

New York Toronto London Auckland
Sydney Mexico City New Delhi Hong Kong

The Fairyland Palace
Bands
MALL
Wetherbury College
New Harmony Mall
The Village Hall
The Warehouse
Willow Hill

Jack Frost's Ice Castle
The Park
High Street
MUSIC
The Alley
Kirsty's House
Fields
Wetherbury Hotel

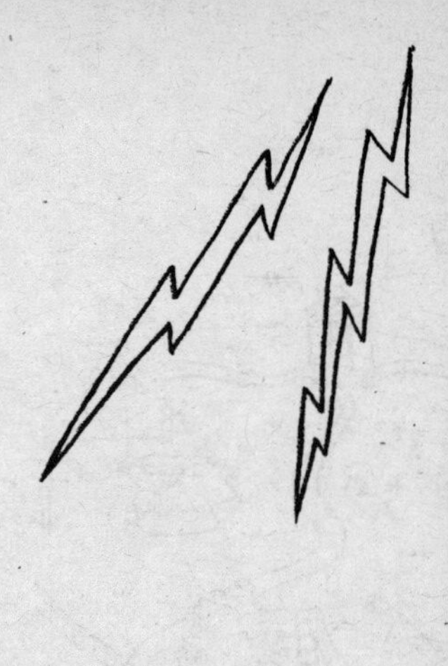

I'm through with frost, ice, and snow.
To the human world I must go!
I'll form my cool Gobolicious Band.
Magical instruments will lend a hand.

With these instruments, I'll go far.
Frosty Jack, a superstar.
I'll steal music's harmony and its fun.
Watch out, world, I'll be number one!

Contents

Guitar Star! 1

A Goblin in Disguise? 15

Making Music 25

A Goblin Trap 35

Splat! 45

Catch That Guitar! 55

Rachel Walker smiled across the breakfast table at her best friend, Kirsty Tate. "Yesterday was a really great start to school break, wasn't it?" she said. "I love spending our vacations together. We always have the best adventures!"

Rachel was staying with Kirsty's family for the whole week of break. The two

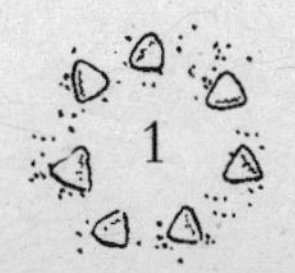

girls had been friends for a long time, and just yesterday they had made some new friends — the Music Fairies!

Kirsty nodded. "It was so exciting meeting Poppy the Piano Fairy, and helping her get her magic piano back from the goblins. I loved it when —" She stopped suddenly. "Did you hear something?" she asked.

The two girls sat in silence for a moment, listening. Nobody, not even their parents, knew about their fairy friends, and the girls were careful to keep it that way. It was their most special secret! The two of them had been to Fairyland many times now, helping many kinds of different fairies and having some very magical adventures.

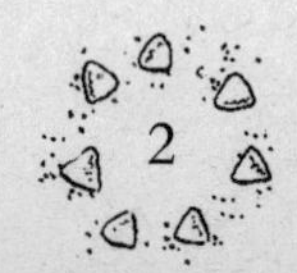

Kirsty and Rachel could both hear footsteps approaching — and another noise, too.

"It sounds like bells," Rachel said in surprise. "Or a tambourine!" Her eyes lit up as she turned to Kirsty. "Do you think it's a magic musical instrument?"

Yesterday, the girls had discovered that Jack Frost, a very mischievous fairy, had stolen all seven of the Music Fairies' magic musical instruments. He wanted to form a pop group with his goblins — Frosty and his Gobolicious Band. Jack Frost was hoping his band would win the National Talent Competition that was being held in Wetherbury at the end of the week, but the fairies couldn't let that happen. If he did win, it wouldn't take long for people to figure out that he wasn't human. And once the world knew that fairies really existed, all of Kirsty and Rachel's magical friends would be in danger of being discovered by nosy, meddling humans!

Kirsty, Rachel, and Poppy had managed to find the magic piano

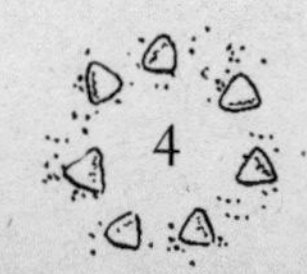

yesterday, but there were still six other missing magic instruments that had to be tracked down.

"I don't remember there being a magic tambourine," Kirsty replied in a low voice, looking puzzled. Then the kitchen door opened, and her face broke into a grin. "Dad — it's you!"

Mr. Tate came into the room, shaking a tambourine enthusiastically. "Morning,

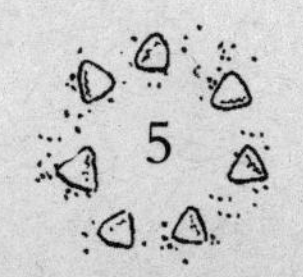

girls!" he said cheerfully. He went over to the table, grabbed a piece of toast, and waved good-bye with his tambourine as he walked back to the door.

"Do you have band practice now?" Kirsty asked.

Mr. Tate grinned. "I sure do," he said. "Your uncle John's already out there warming up on the drums, and Dave just arrived, too." He smiled at Rachel. "Your ears are in for a treat, girls!"

Kirsty laughed as he left the room. "I wouldn't call it a treat," she told Rachel. "They're not very good. And now that the fairies' instruments are missing, Dad's band is going to sound even worse than usual!"

The two girls had learned yesterday that the Music Fairies used their magic musical instruments to help make playing music fun. The instruments also ensured that music sounded harmonious all around the world. Ever since the goblins had taken the magic instruments, music was sounding flat and tuneless everywhere. It was far less enjoyable to play — and to hear!

"Your dad's band can't be that bad," Rachel said, getting to her feet. "Let's go and listen."

The two girls left the kitchen and went out to the barn that stood a short distance from the Tates' house. They

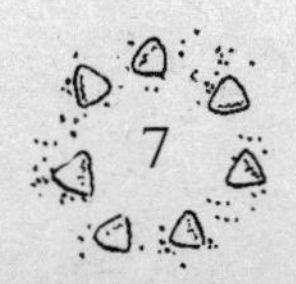

peeked around the door to see Mr. Tate playing an electric keyboard with one hand and shaking a tambourine with the other. Kirsty's uncle John was pounding on the drums, and a third man was taking off his jacket. A guitar case was propped up next to him.

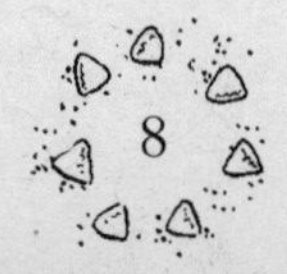

"What a mess!" Kirsty whispered to Rachel. "We've got to find those other missing instruments. This is one band that really needs help!"

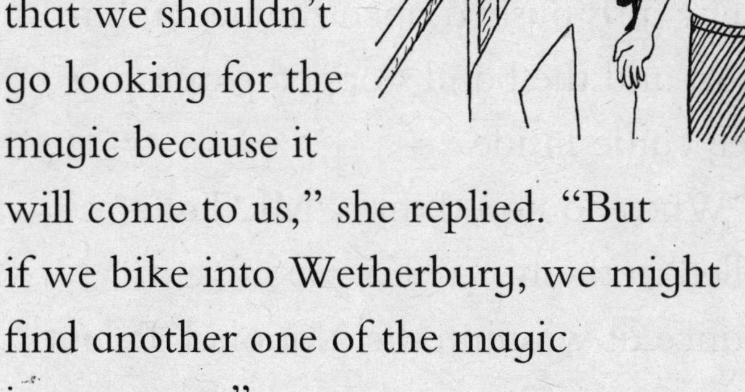

Rachel had to agree. "I know the fairies always say that we shouldn't go looking for the magic because it will come to us," she replied. "But if we bike into Wetherbury, we might find another one of the magic instruments."

"Good idea," Kirsty said. "The bikes are in the barn. Follow me!"

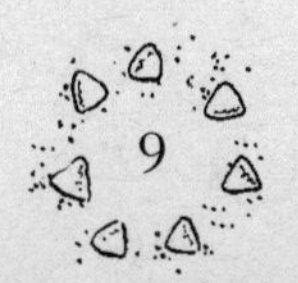

The girls pushed open the heavy barn door, and the band stopped playing as they came inside.

"What do you think?" Mr. Tate called to them. "Think we have a chance at winning the National Talent Competition?"

"You never know," Rachel said with a smile.

"We won't win anything if we can't

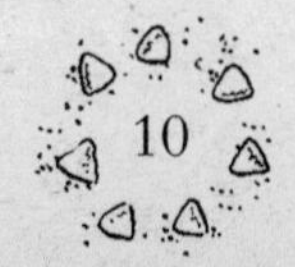

keep time," Kirsty's uncle grumbled, setting down his drumsticks with a sigh. "Sorry, guys. I don't know what's wrong with me today. I totally lost the beat there."

The two girls exchanged glances. They knew why John was struggling — it was all because of the missing magic instruments. They had to find the rest of them — and fast!

"Don't worry," Kirsty's dad said. "Let's practice an easier one next. How about . . . ?" He shuffled through a stack of paper, and the men started discussing lyrics and chord changes.

Kirsty went to get the bikes and accidentally

bumped into Dave's guitar case. It fell to the ground with a thud, and popped open.

"Oh no!" Kirsty cried, bending down.

The men were so engrossed in their discussion that they hadn't even noticed.

Kirsty was about to pick up the guitar when the hole in the middle started

glowing. Rachel walked over to take a closer look. "Is it broken?" she whispered anxiously.

But before Kirsty could reply, there was a faint strumming sound — and out flew Ellie the Guitar Fairy!

A Goblin in Disguise?

The girls recognized the little fairy from when they'd met all of the Music Fairies the day before. They were excited to see her again! Ellie was wearing a short blue skirt with sequins on the waistband. She also had on a striped tank, leggings, and sporty high-tops. Her dark hair bobbed around her face as she flew up to the girls.

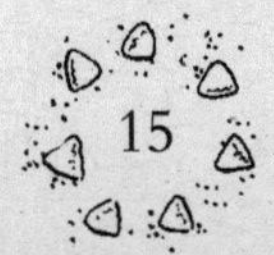

“Hello there!” she said cheerfully.

Kirsty glanced over her shoulder to where her dad and his friends were still talking. She didn’t want them to notice Ellie! “Hi,” she said in a low voice. “We’d better get you out of here before anyone sees you.”

"Of course," Ellie agreed. She flicked her wand at the guitar case, which quietly closed itself. Then she fluttered under Rachel's hair.

Kirsty and Rachel walked quickly out of the barn. "I heard some awful music — that's why I came," Ellie explained. "And now that I'm here, I have a strong feeling that my magic guitar is somewhere nearby."

"We'll help you look for it," Rachel said, gazing around.

"But your magic guitar might not even be enough to make my dad's band sound better," Kirsty said, grinning. "That was the awful music you heard."

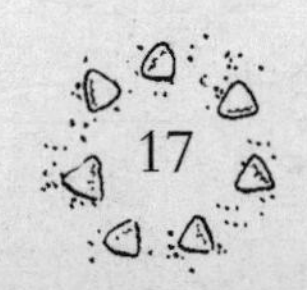

"Oops," Ellie said, with a tinkling laugh. She fluttered off Rachel's shoulder and hovered in midair, her beating wings a blur of shimmering color. "Let's start looking anyway, all right? Where would a goblin have hidden my guitar?"

The three friends were just about to start searching in the yard when a short, stocky man came up the front walk. Kirsty gazed at him with curiosity. He was wearing a cowboy hat, a long leather coat, and enormous sunglasses.

Ellie darted behind the girls as the man walked up.

"Where's the band practicing?" he

asked in a high, squeaky voice. "I'm the lead singer."

Kirsty's heart thumped. The man was very short — could he be a goblin? With his hat and sunglasses it was hard to tell. Kirsty pointed to the barn, too shocked to speak.

"Are you thinking what I'm thinking?" Rachel whispered as the man moved out of earshot.

Kirsty nodded. "I've never seen him before," she replied. "He might be a goblin!"

Ellie raised her eyebrows, unbelieving. "No!" she said. "Goblins are green. You two should know that by now!"

Rachel shook her head. "We found out

that Jack Frost has cast a spell over the goblins to make them blend in with the humans," she told Ellie. "The goblin we saw yesterday wasn't green at all."

"He still had big goblin ears and feet," Kirsty said, "and a long, pointy nose. That was how we knew he wasn't really human."

"Let's take a closer look at this singer," Ellie said eagerly, and the three of them went back toward the barn.

As they got closer, the girls could hear the new arrival singing in a loud, screechy voice. "He is *so* bad," Kirsty whispered in horror. She peeked around the barn door, trying to see the singer's feet. Were they huge goblin feet? It was hard to tell with the cowboy boots he was wearing.

Kirsty tried to sneak closer for a better look, but was nearly knocked in the head by her uncle John's drumsticks as he played. Then Rachel tripped on the electric cable from the keyboard!

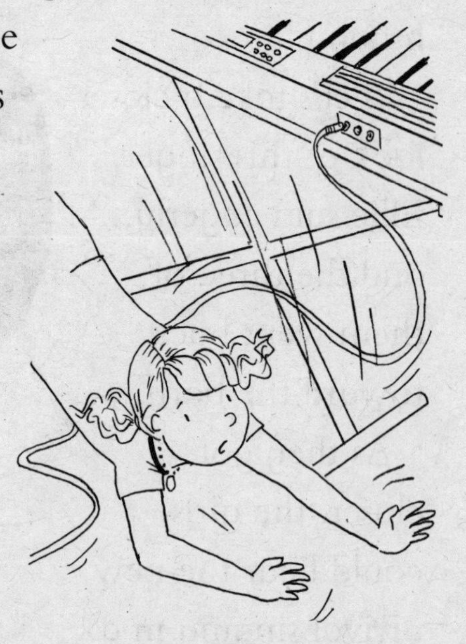

The man in the cowboy hat

stopped singing and turned toward her, and Rachel gasped nervously. Oh no! She'd been caught spying! If the singer really was a goblin, he'd be suspicious for sure. . . .

Making Music

The singer reached out a hand to help Rachel to her feet and smiled at her. "Are you OK?" he asked.

Rachel blushed. "Yes, thanks," she said. Her mind was racing. She knew that goblins were usually very rude. But this man had just been kind to her!

“Sorry,” she went on. “I was just looking for a bike helmet.”

“No problem,” the singer said, tipping his hat to her.

With his hat off, Rachel, Kirsty, and Ellie all got a good look at the singer’s face. He had normal ears and an ordinary nose. He wasn’t a goblin at all!

“Here are the helmets,” Kirsty said, handing one to Rachel. “And here’s a bike you can borrow.”

The girls quickly wheeled the bikes out of the barn. “That was my fault,” Kirsty said. “I should have guessed the singer wasn’t a goblin. My dad and the rest of the band all knew him!”

“Never mind,” Rachel said. “We —” Then she stopped. “Hey,” she said, listening. “It actually sounds like the band is playing OK now. They seem to be getting the hang of it.”

Ellie nodded. “And that electric guitar really rocks!” she added.

Kirsty frowned. “But they don’t have an electric guitar,” she said. “Dave’s guitar is an old acoustic one, remember?”

They looked at one another. “So

where is that guitar music coming from?" Rachel asked, feeling excited.

They listened again. "This way," Ellie decided, pointing ahead. The girls left their bikes propped up and followed the sound to the back of the barn. They glimpsed around the corner to see a small figure with a bandana on his head, wearing a leather jacket. He was perched on the wall, with an electric guitar slung over his shoulder.

He wasn't green — but there was no mistaking the size and shape of his goblin ears! Ellie clapped her hands in excitement. "That's my guitar!" she whispered. "It's much bigger than its usual Fairyland size, but it's definitely mine."

The goblin finished playing, and Ellie darted behind Rachel's back as he looked up. He saw the girls watching him and bowed his head. "I'd love to stay longer, but I've got places to go," he said grandly.

"Oh, that's too bad," Rachel said. "Can't you play some more?" She didn't want the goblin to disappear before they thought of a way to get Ellie's guitar back. "I was really enjoying

listening to that song. You're such a great musician."

The goblin smiled, flattered by all the praise. "Well," he said, "maybe I could stay a little longer. . . ."

"Good job, Rachel," Ellie whispered from her hiding place.

The goblin bent over the guitar and began to play. Seeing him picking out the notes gave Kirsty an idea. "Would you mind showing me a few chords?" she asked him. "I've always wanted to learn to play the guitar, and you're the best player I've ever heard."

The goblin raised his chin and gave Kirsty a smug grin. "It's true," he agreed. "I *am* the best player in the world. I'm the lead guitarist for Frosty and his Gobolicious Band, you know.

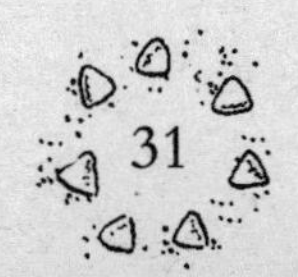

Remember that name," he told them. "You're going to be hearing a lot more about our band very soon."

Kirsty sat next to him on the wall and watched as he demonstrated a few chords. He couldn't resist showing off with some fancy fingerwork, making the guitar's music ring out in the cool morning air.

"Wow," Kirsty said. "Can I try now?" She reached out a hand to take the guitar. She planned to snatch it and give it straight to Ellie — but the goblin yanked the guitar away from her! "Nobody touches this but me," he said sternly.

Rachel could hear Ellie giving a quiet little *tsk tsk* from behind her. And then it seemed that the fairy wasn't able to hold

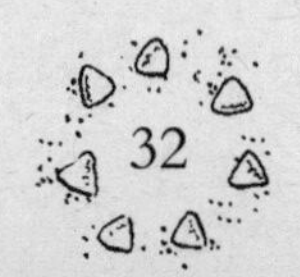

in her frustration anymore. Suddenly, she soared out of her hiding place and hovered in front of the goblin. She had her hands firmly on her hips. "It's not yours, it's mine," she said angrily. "And I want it back — now!"

Ellie flew straight for the guitar, her fingers reaching for one of the tuning pegs. The goblin tried to bat her away with the neck of the guitar. Ellie had to dodge it quickly to avoid being hit!

Then the goblin backed away from the girls. "I'm going," he said, "and don't waste my time trying to trick me anymore. I'm off to the Wetherbury Music Store. Bye!"

"Wait!" Kirsty called out, desperate for him to stay. "The Wetherbury Music Store? Why are you going there?" she asked.

The goblin had already stormed off in a huffy way, but he couldn't resist turning around again. "Because the so-called best guitarist in the human world — Heddie Van Walen — is signing his latest CD there today. But

now that *I'm* the best guitarist in Fairyland *and* the human world, I'm going to show Heddie a thing or two."

He turned on his heel and started off again.

"Wait," Rachel shouted out. "You can't just go into town. You're a goblin! Someone will figure it out!"

The goblin put his nose in the air. "Silly girl," he sniffed. "Thanks to Jack Frost's spell, I look like a human now. No one will ever suspect *me* of being a goblin!"

The girls exchanged glances. The goblin might not be green anymore, but he still didn't exactly look human.

The goblin dashed past them to the barn, where he grabbed Kirsty's bike. He slung the guitar around his back, jumped on the bike, and pedaled off.

"Hey! Come back here with that!" Kirsty shouted, but it was too late. The goblin had already vanished into the distance.

Rachel sighed in frustration. "Now we only have one bike between us," she said.

"You ride the bike, I'll run," Kirsty suggested.

Ellie shook her head. "I've got a better idea," she said, and waved her wand over them both. Bright blue fairy dust spiraled out from the tip of her wand, and the girls immediately shrank down to fairy size. Delicate wings appeared on their backs.

Kirsty beamed and zoomed up into the air. Oh, how she loved being a fairy! "Now we can all fly after the goblin," she said. "Good thinking, Ellie!"

The three fairies set off toward Wetherbury. Kirsty showed them a shortcut over the

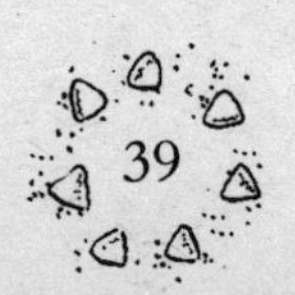

fields so that the goblin wouldn't see them following him. It only took a few minutes for them to reach the music store in town. They perched on the store's sign and searched around for the goblin — but couldn't see him anywhere.

"I think we beat him here," Ellie said. "That gives us some time to think and to come up with a plan."

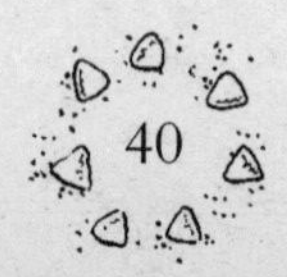

Rachel fluttered into the air to look around the side of the shop. "There's an alley down here," she told the others. "A dead end. It would be good if we could trap the goblin there somehow."

"How could we lure him into an alley?" Kirsty wondered, coming to see. "Maybe we could make some kind of sign that would tempt him down there?"

"Yes," said Rachel. "And then, once we've got him trapped, we'll have a better chance of getting the magic guitar back."

"And my bike!" Kirsty added.

"Great," Ellie said, brightening at the thought. "I'd better turn you back into girls," she decided, and waved her wand over them.

Glittering blue fairy dust floated all around them, and Kirsty and Rachel felt themselves getting bigger again.

"And maybe we could use something like this, too?" Ellie went on, and waved her wand a second time. Kirsty and Rachel watched in delight as a sparkling, flashing sign

appeared on the side of the music store, with an arrow pointing down the alley. It read LEAD GUITARISTS THIS WAY!

Kirsty giggled. "Perfect," she said. "He won't be able to resist!"

"And just in time, too," Rachel added, spotting a figure coming up High Street on a familiar bicycle. "Here he comes — hide!"

Kirsty and Rachel darted behind a trash can, with Ellie flying behind them. "Ugh, it stinks," Kirsty grumbled, fanning a hand in front of her face. "I think this must be the back of the market — look at all those crates of rotten fruit."

The girls and Ellie could see oranges covered with green mold, squishy bruised

apples, and slimy grapes piled up in boxes. "Yuck," Rachel commented. "No wonder they were thrown out."

"Here comes the goblin," whispered Ellie, spying from behind the can. The girls peeked out too, and saw him getting off Kirsty's bike and reading the neon sign. "*Lead Guitarists This Way*?" he said to himself in a pleased sort of voice. "That's me!"

He pushed the bike between two trash cans near the end of the alley. He wasn't really watching where he was going and

walked straight into a Dumpster. An alley cat let out a frightened *meow* from the top of the Dumpster, and then leaped off with its claws outstretched. The goblin screamed and jumped back, startled. The bike clattered to the ground.

Kirsty watched as the goblin struggled with the bike. She was trying to think of a way to get the guitar back, but it was hard to concentrate when the air was heavy with the smell of rotten fruit. Fruit . . . Of course! Maybe they could use the fruit!

"Ellie," she whispered, "if you could sneak behind the goblin, he might run further into the alley to get away from you. Then Rachel and I can pelt him with this rotten fruit!"

Rachel sputtered with giggles and had to clap a hand over her mouth to keep quiet. Ellie's eyes were bright with mischief. "I love it," the little fairy said. "Get ready, girls. I'll send him your way!"

Ellie zoomed to the end of the alley, high up in the air so the goblin wouldn't notice. Luckily, he was still messing with the bike, so he didn't spot her. Then Ellie flew behind him. "OK," she yelled. "Now I can get my guitar back!"

The goblin jumped when he heard her and swung around. "Oh, no you can't!" he insisted, racing down the alley toward Rachel and Kirsty's hiding place.

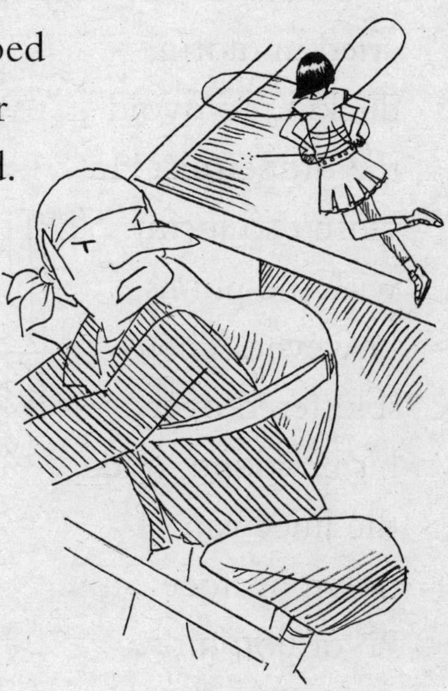

The plan was working! Both girls grabbed armfuls of fruit from a nearby crate and began throwing it at the goblin. *Zing*! There went a moldy grapefruit! And a bunch of soggy plums!

"Aaargh!" the goblin cried in alarm, ducking to avoid the grapefruit. He wasn't so lucky with the plums, however. They splattered over his bandana, and the juice ran down his face. "Not you girls again!" he raged, trying to wipe it out of his eyes. He took the guitar off his back and held it high, so that none of the fruit would hit it. "You're not getting my guitar that easily," he told them.

The goblin glanced behind him, back the way he'd come. Rachel knew he was thinking about trying to escape. Her gaze fell upon a box of overripe bananas, and she knew just what to do.

"Ellie! Could you use your magic to scatter these around his feet?" she directed.

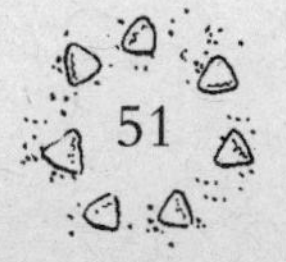

Ellie grinned from where she was floating in midair. "No problem!" She waved her wand. With a stream of sparkling blue fairy dust, the bananas whizzed out of the box and landed on the ground all around the goblin.

Kirsty figured out her friend's plan and grabbed some giant watermelons. She rolled them straight at the goblin like big green bowling balls.

The goblin jumped high over one of the melons, but landed on a slippery banana that splurted under his foot and made him skid. "Whooaaaa!" he cried. He tumbled over, letting go of Ellie's magic guitar . . . and sending it flying through the air!

Catch That Guitar!

The girls raced out from their hiding place and dodged all the bananas, hoping to catch the guitar. Meanwhile, the goblin had fallen with a giant splat onto a pile of fruit. He slithered around in the slime as he tried to get up.

Ellie tossed a handful of fairy dust at the guitar as it fell. The blue dust

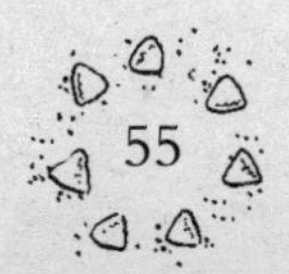

sparkled like glitter in the sunshine, swirling all around the instrument. There was a puff of blue smoke, and then the guitar shrank to its Fairyland size, and floated down gently.

Rachel reached out and caught it before it fell to the ground.

"Got it!" she cheered.

The goblin scrambled to his feet, slipping and sliding on

the squashed bananas. He howled with rage. "Give that back!" he yelled, lunging for Rachel.

Before the goblin could reach her, Ellie swooped down and Rachel passed the magic guitar up to the little fairy.

"Thank you!" Ellie cried in delight. As she soared up high, she plucked the guitar's strings lovingly. "Oh, it's so good to have this back again!"

The goblin glared at her, and jumped up and down, trying to snatch the guitar. "I want that back," he wailed. "How

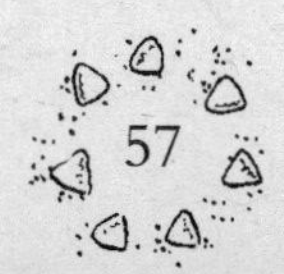

can I be lead guitarist without my guitar?"

Ellie looked down at him. "You know, these magic instruments are supposed to help *everyone* enjoy music," she told him. "I need to take this guitar back to Fairyland where it belongs. But there's nothing to stop you from getting your own guitar to play — it would still be fun!"

The goblin stamped his foot. "But I want to be better than Heddie Van Walen," he grumbled.

"Then you need to practice," Ellie told him. "And I need to do some cleaning up here," she added, gazing around the alley. She played a funky little tune on her magic guitar and sang:

"All you fruits down in the street, put yourselves back, to make things neat!"

There was a flash of blue light in the alley. All the scattered fruit sailed up into the air and returned to the crates.

The sign at the front of the alley that read LEAD GUITARISTS THIS WAY! also disappeared in a cloud of blue glitter.

"There!" Ellie smiled. "That's better. Now *you're* the only thing making this

place look messy," she said to the goblin. "I think you'd better go back to Fairyland, don't you?"

The goblin took off his bandana, wiped the plum juice from his face, and walked away in defeat.

"Wow," Rachel said, looking around the alley. It looked exactly like it did when they arrived. No one would ever be able to tell there had just been a fruit-fight with a goblin there. "I wish I

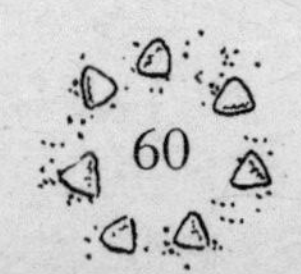

knew a song like that to clean up my bedroom!"

Ellie giggled. "Girls, you did a great job helping me get my guitar back," she said to them, flying down to kiss them each on the cheek. Her wings tickled against Rachel's face.

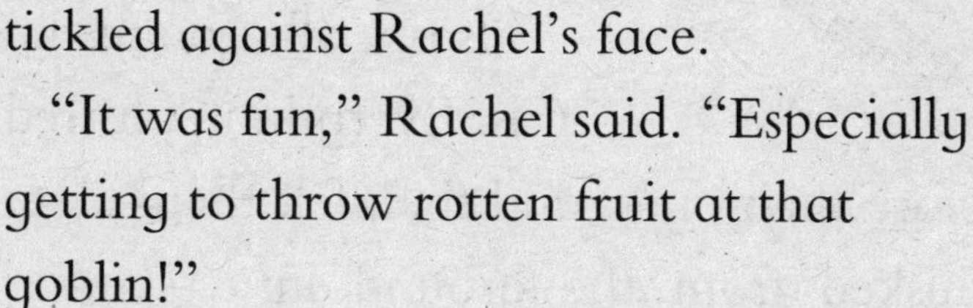

"It was fun," Rachel said. "Especially getting to throw rotten fruit at that goblin!"

"I guess we should go home now," Kirsty said, "and see if Dad's band is any better, now that you've got your guitar back."

Ellie smiled. "I'll return to Fairyland

just as soon as I've sent you home with a little magic," she said. "I hope you'll hear an improvement in their music. Good-bye!"

She waved her wand in a swirly pattern, and streams of glittery fairy dust whooshed from its tip, all around the girls. Everything blurred before their eyes, and they felt themselves whisked from the ground in a sparkly whirlwind, with the faint sound of Ellie's funky guitar in their ears. Then they felt themselves land again, and they opened their eyes.

They were outside the barn at Kirsty's house, and the bike that the goblin had borrowed was safely back with them, too. They could just hear the sound of Mr. Tate's band. To their surprise, they seemed to be playing in tune now! The girls noticed a strong guitar strum leading the song.

"Ellie's guitar magic really is amazing," Kirsty said, listening. "They actually sound pretty good!"

Rachel grinned. "Maybe they should enter the National Talent Competition after all," she joked.

Kirsty nodded. "First, we've got to stop Jack Frost from winning it with his band," she reminded her friend. "There are five magic instruments left to find — and only five days until the competition."

"It's going to be a busy week," Rachel said. "And a very musical one, too, I hope!"

THE MUSIC FAIRIES

Ellie the Guitar Fairy has her magic instrument back! Now Rachel and Kirsty must help

Fiona the Flute Fairy!

Join their next adventure in this special sneak peek. . . .

"Oh, this is one of my favorite stores in Wetherbury!" Rachel Walker stopped outside Sparkly Wishes and turned to her best friend, Kirsty Tate. "They always have such fabulous cards and gifts. Can we go in?"

"OK," Kirsty agreed, pushing open the shop door. "Do you want to buy something or just look around?"

"I want to get a thank-you card to give to your parents when I go home at the end of school break," Rachel replied, as they went inside.

Kirsty smiled, "Oh, that's so nice, Rachel!"

Suddenly Kirsty spotted a large, bright card at the front of a nearby display. The card was covered with silver sparkles, and a pretty little fairy with long red hair was in the middle.

She looks like Poppy the Piano Fairy! Kirsty thought.

Kirsty took the card to show Rachel, who was looking at postcards of various Wetherbury sights.

"Does this remind you of anyone, Rachel?" asked Kirsty, holding the card out.

"Oh yes — Poppy!" Rachel exclaimed. "Maybe I should send that card to my mom and dad. What does it say inside, Kirsty?"

Kirsty flipped the card open. Immediately a puff of glitter burst out, showering both girls with sparkles. Rachel and Kirsty gasped as a tiny fairy popped out of the card and waved at them. She wore a shiny silver dress with lace-up sandals, and her dark hair was braided with beads.

"Hi, girls," she called. "I'm Fiona the Flute Fairy!"

"We're so glad to see you, Fiona," Rachel said eagerly.

"Do you think your magic flute is nearby?" asked Kirsty.

Fiona nodded solemnly. "And I hope you'll help me find it," she went on. "There's no time to waste!"